# A TAXI DOG

# CHRISTMAS

Published by Dial Books for Young Readers
A Division of Penguin Books USA Inc.
375 Hudson Street
New York, New York 10014

Library of Congress Cataloging in Publication Data
Barracca, Debra.  A taxi dog Christmas/by Debra and Sal Barracca;
pictures by Alan Ayers.

p.  cm.
Summary: Maxi and Jim the taxi driver gladly interrupt their Christmas
celebration to lend Santa a hand.
ISBN 0-8037-1360-6 (tr.).—ISBN 0-8037-1361-4 (lib.)
[1. Dogs—Fiction. 2. Christmas—Fiction. 3. Taxicabs—Fiction.
4. Stories in rhyme.]
I. Barracca, Sal. II. Ayers, Alan, ill. III. Title.
PZ8.3.B25263Tax 1994 [E]—dc20 91-44953 CIP AC

*The art for this book was prepared by using oil paints.
It was then color-separated and reproduced in red, yellow, blue, and black halftones.*

*For Samantha, our own little miracle*
D.B. and S.B.


*For Megan Elaine Wagman*
A.A.

I awoke with a yawn
   At the first light of dawn.
      To the window so softly I crept.
I saw with delight
   That a blanket of white
      Had covered the ground while we slept.

"Come on, Jim, let's go!
    It's late now, you know."
        "All right," he said, "hold on there, Maxi—
Today's Christmas Eve,
    We don't have to leave
        Until later to pick up our taxi."

A knock at the door,
In burst Mrs. Shore
With fresh homemade cookies and bread.
Jim didn't know
That she'd brought mistletoe,
And she kissed him until he turned red.

We all trimmed the tree
   And sang carols (off-key).
      A fire was blazing so brightly.
The popcorn was strung
   And the stockings were hung.
      Outside, snow fluttered down lightly.

We braved the cold weather
And working together,
We built a big dog out of snow.
With a scarf of bright red
And a cap on his head,
He looked just like someone we know!

We dodged a snowplow,
    Then we heard a "Meow."
        I perked up my ears at the sound.
We followed the cry
    To an alley nearby,
        And six cold, hungry kittens we found.

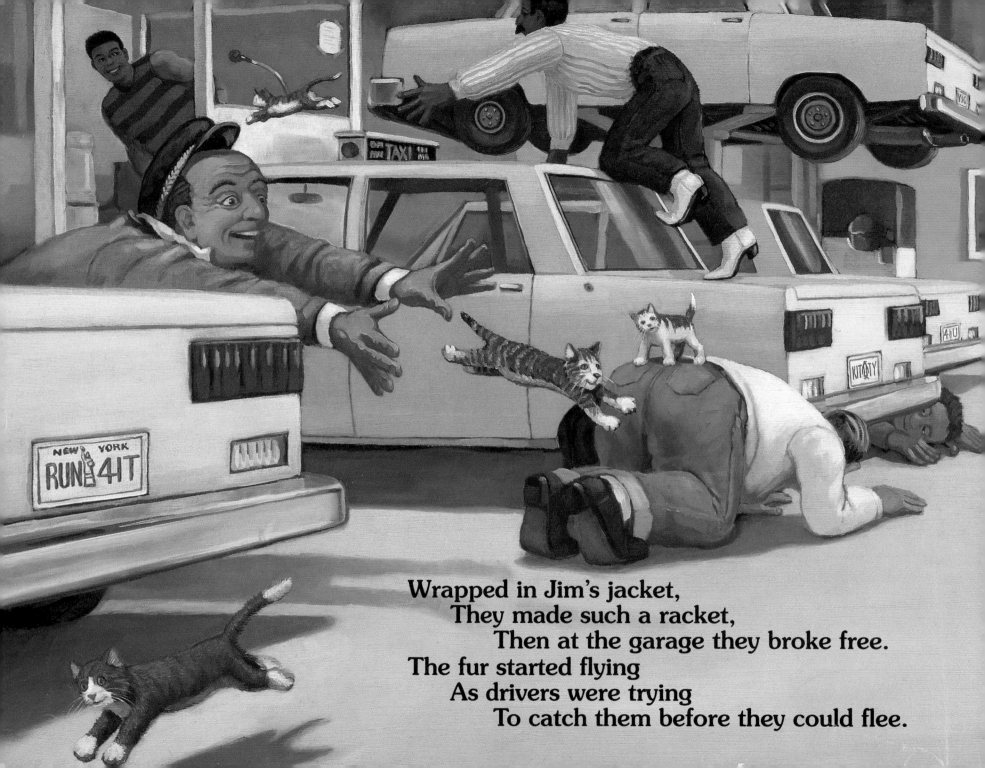

Wrapped in Jim's jacket,
They made such a racket,
Then at the garage they broke free.
The fur started flying
As drivers were trying
To catch them before they could flee.

Then each lucky tabby
    Went home with a cabbie,
        Except one who wanted to play.
She started to purr
    As I licked her soft fur.
        We knew she was going to stay.

With our new little kitty
    We drove through the city
        To start on our holiday shift.
Store windows were glowing,
    The streets overflowing
        With shoppers who sought one last gift.

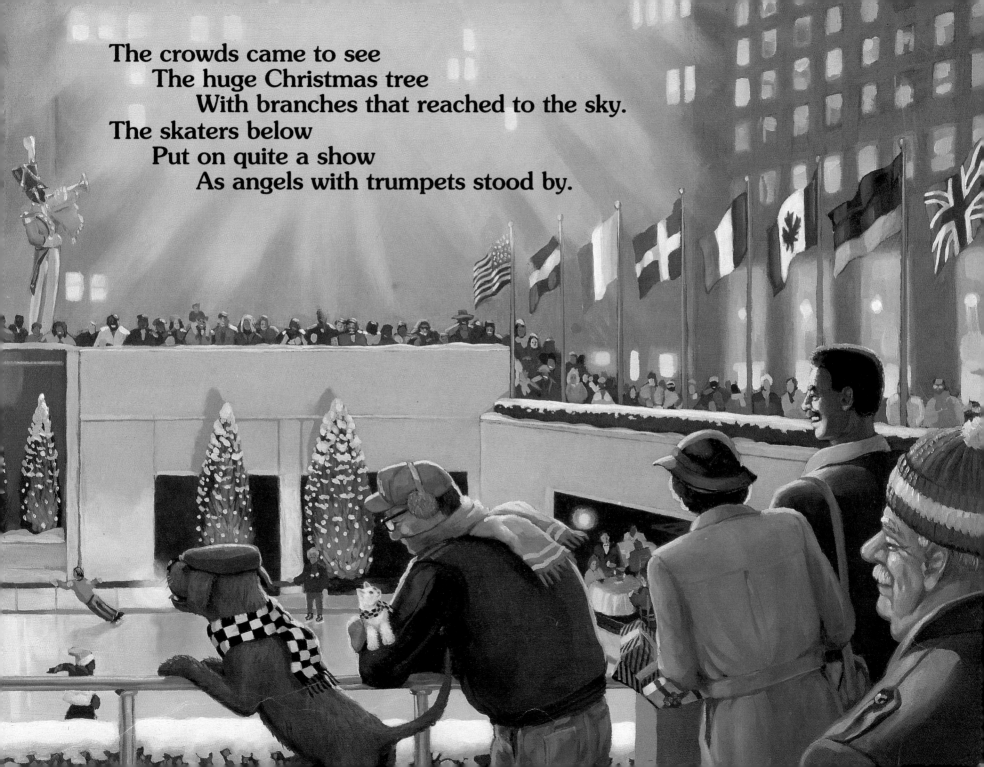

The crowds came to see
    The huge Christmas tree
        With branches that reached to the sky.
The skaters below
    Put on quite a show
        As angels with trumpets stood by.

Jim rented some skates
  And he made figure eights;
    He jumped and then twirled on his toes.
He spun like a top,
  Then came to a stop
    As I slid 'round the ice on my nose.

The church bells were ringing.
We all joined in singing
The sweet sounds of "O, Holy Night."
Then we heard, "Ho! Ho! Ho!,
Look out, down below!"
What we saw gave us all such a fright!

Right at our feet
Santa crashed to the street.
Upon landing, his sleigh split in two.
"I lost flight control
When I left the North Pole,"
Santa said. "What on earth shall I do?"

Dazzled and dazed,
  We stood there amazed
    At the toys on the ground that were scattered.
Dolls, ducks, and trains,
  And pianos and planes,
    And a rainbow of paints wildly splattered.

Santa said, "Let me think...."
     Then he gave us a wink
          When he looked at our bright yellow taxi.
"It's perfectly clear,
     What I need is right here.
          Will you help me, please, Jim and Maxi?"

"Let's hurry," he cried
　　As the reindeer were tied
　　　　To the front of his new taxi sleigh.
He then touched my nose,
　　And up, up we rose....

Together we saved Christmas Day.

And so on that night
      Our taxi took flight
            To deliver the toys Christmas Eve.
Some say it's not so,
      But as all children know,
            In your heart you just have to believe.